The Berenstain Bears
and the
TROUBLE WITH
CHORES

When asked to do something
that they hate,
most bears will
procrastinate.

THINGS TO DO

Set the table
Clear away dishes
Empty waste baskets
Put out trash
Cut grass
Coil garden hose
Clean up messy room
Empty vacuum
Pick up toys
Rake leaves
Sweep steps

The Berenstain Bears
and the
TROUBLE WITH
CHORES

Stan & Jan Berenstain

HarperFestival®
A Division of HarperCollins*Publishers*

The Berenstain Bears and the Trouble with Chores
Copyright © 2005 by Berenstain Bears, Inc.
HarperCollins®, ♣®, and HarperFestival® are trademarks of HarperCollins Publishers Inc. Manufactured in China.
10 East 53rd Street, New York, NY 10022.
www.harperchildrens.com
Library of Congress catalog card number: 2004023106
13 14 SCP 30 29 28 27 26 25 24 23
❖

Brother and Sister Bear were good about most things.

They kept up with their schoolwork.

They wore their safety helmets when they went biking and skateboarding.

They said "please" and "thank you" without being prompted.

Papa Bear was good about most things, too.
He helped the cubs with their homework.

He kept his tools sharp and shipshape.

He was always ready to help a neighbor.

But there was one thing the cubs and Papa were not good about—that was chores.

It wasn't that Papa and the cubs didn't want to do their chores. It was just that they always seemed to have reasons not to do them.

And they had such good excuses.

"You're right, my dear," said Papa. "The grass does need cutting. But a mama spider has spun a wonderful web on the lawn mower and I haven't the heart to put all her hard work to waste."

"Mama," said Brother, "may I skip setting the table tonight? There's a TV show on the ice age, and I have to do a report on the Beast of Baluchistan."

"Mama," said Sister, "I know it's my week to clean up Little Lady's calling cards. It's just that I'm waiting for them to dry. They'll be easier to scoop up that way."

There was also the endless bickering about who did what.

"Why is it," complained Sister, "that Brother gets the easy jobs, like setting the table, and I get the yucky ones, like scraping the plates into the garbage?"

"Easy? *Easy?*" protested Brother. "Setting that table is hard! You've got to remember where everything goes—the knives, the spoons, the forks!"

"Wanna trade?" asked Sister. "No, thanks," said Brother. So it went: argue, argue, bicker, bicker.

Mama sighed.

If only Papa and the cubs were as good at doing their chores as they were at arguing about them, life would be a lot easier.

And speaking of easier, thought Mama, *instead of nagging them about chores, it would be a lot easier to do them myself.*

And that's what she did.
    She set and cleared the table.

She cleaned up after
Little Lady.

She chased the dust
bunnies from under
the furniture.

There was also baby Honey
to take care of—

not to mention the cubs' messy room.

The cubs did pick up and put away—
sometimes.

Papa did cut the grass—
occasionally.

And the cubs did chase
the dust bunnies—
once in a while.

But when it comes to chores—
sometimes, occasionally, and
once in a while don't count.

Not surprisingly, things began to slide. Everybody got a little grouchy—especially Mama.

Something had to be done. But what?

Papa decided to call a family meeting. "My dear," he said. "I've been thinking."

"Yes?" said Mama.

"What I've been thinking," he continued, "is that we might want to relax a bit, to ease up on the chores a little."

"Oh?" said Mama.

"Yes," said Papa. "There's a lot more to life than chores. There's walking in the sunshine, enjoying Mother Nature, and fishing in the old fishing hole."

"There's riding bikes," said Brother.

"And jumping rope," said Sister.

Then, to Papa and the cubs' great surprise, Mama said, "You know something? I think you're absolutely right."

"You do?" said Papa.

"I certainly do," said Mama with a sly gleam in her eye. "I've been so concerned with the house that I haven't been to my quilting club for weeks. And with the flower show coming up, I should be preparing my exhibit."

Not worrying about spiderwebs and dust bunnies worked pretty well at first. There were a few bad moments—like when baby Honey almost ate a bug.

But Mama was her smiling self again. She got back into quilting and began work on her flower show exhibit. "I was thinking of combining Shasta daisies and Silver Moon roses. What do you think, dear?" she asked.

"Sounds fine to me," said Papa, who was working on his fishing gear.

"Mama," said Sister. "I'm growing this grapefruit plant for school and there are so many dishes in the kitchen sink that I can't water it."

"No problem," said Mama. "Just water it in the bathroom upstairs."

Sister stomped upstairs with her grapefruit plant.

"Mama," said Brother, "I left my marbles on the floor and now they're gone!"

"Goodness!" said Mama. "I must have sucked them up with the vacuum. I do have to vacuum once in a while."

"But one of them was my best shooter!" said Brother.

"Oh, I'm sure you can find them by emptying the vacuum bag," said Mama.

"But . . . but . . . but . . ." sputtered Brother.

"Now if you'll excuse me," said Mama. "I'm off to my quilting club."

Some household tasks got done. Beds got made—more or less. Meals got served—sort of. But bit by bit, messy build-up began to take over the tree house.

Wet towels piled up in the bathroom.

Fruit flies hovered over dishes in the kitchen sink.

The pictures on the wall got crookeder and crookeder, and there was a whole army of dust bunnies under the sofa.

There were so many burnt crumbs
in the bottom of the toaster oven
that the whole kitchen smelled
burnt.

A strange green mold
grew on the shower curtain,

and a thousand-legger came swimming
toward Sister in the bathtub.

Yes, Brother was having fun riding his bike. Sister was having fun jumping rope.

Papa brought home some fine fish, and Mama finished her beautiful new quilt.

But living in all that messy build-up wasn't much fun. And one day when Mama was off at the garden club, Papa decided to call another meeting. No sooner had the meeting been called to order than everybody was talking at once—and they were all saying the same thing: "WE'VE GOT TO DO SOMETHING ABOUT THIS AWFUL MESS!"

And they did.

They picked up all the wet towels.

They got the dishes out of the sink.

They straightened the pictures.

They cleaned out the toaster oven, banished the dust bunnies, and scrubbed the shower curtain. Then they sat down, exhausted and pleased, and waited for Mama to come home.

"Well," she said when she returned, "everything is set for the flower show. And I think there's a good chance I may win an award." Papa and the cubs waited for her to notice what they had done. But all Mama did was take off her yellow "going out" hat and put on her blue "at home" duster.

"Mama," said Sister, "haven't you noticed anything?"
Mama looked around and smiled. "You mean how the
whole house is neat and clean and all the chores are
done—yes, I noticed."

With that, she gathered the cubs into a big bear
hug and gave Papa a great big kiss.